MY HOT NEIGHBOR

JEWEL ALYSSA

Romance/Erotic

Cover image: Pixabay.com

Cover Design: HRK

This is a work of fiction. Names, places, incidents and characters are the product of the author's imagination or used in a fictitious manner. Any resemblance to actual persons, living or dead is entirely coincidental.

No part of this book may be reproduced, distributed or transmitted in any form or by any means including photocopying recording or any other methods without the permission of the author.

Author can be reached by mail.

Jewelalyssa93writer@gmail.com

<u>WARNING 18+</u>

This book contains mature content, explicit erotic scenes and language.

Widow's Desire

The Snake Goddess

The seduced

Sex is serene

The sorcerer 1

The sorcerer 2

The sorcerer 3

Lust is divine

3 erotic stories

The neighbor

The girl next door

We were ready to go to the airport. My neighbor Augustan was going to Dubai.

He got a job as a manager in a production company. It was a dream job for him.

He had sent hundreds of applications all around the globe before he got his job.

He badly wanted to go to Dubai. All his childhood friends were working there.

He was so happy and yet there was a hit of disappointment in his face. He has to leave his wife here as his visa sanctioned was not a family visa.

Augustan is twenty eight and his wife Nina is twenty five. They were married for five years. But they were not fortunate enough to have a baby yet.

Augustan recently bought the house in our neighborhood. He was living in his ancestral home before.

Both our families became close in the early days itself. I am twenty one, studying for final year Arts in college.

Nina was an amazing beauty. She was slim and tall, even few millimeters taller than Augustan.

She is one or two inches taller to me.

She had a perfectly shaped body. She had green eyes, long nose, red lips. Her neck was a precisely crafted work of a genius.

She mostly wore red dresses which made her fair skin glow more.

She was the subject of chats between my friends. They were all jealous to see me freely interacting with her.

I became close friends with Nina. I had enough freedom to put my arms around her shoulders and walk closer to her gripping our bodies together.

My friends asked me to introduce them to her but I was reluctant. I knew what they wanted. They wanted to fuck her. Their hearts were filled with lust.

I wasn't going to let that happen. She is my favorite friend.

Though it was only friendship between us, I felt much more.

My carnal desires were arising inside me. I felt my body awake with desires.

I didn't know what she was thinking about me. I didn't know how to approach her.

After Augustan left, I became more than a visitor in her house. I became a member of the family.

Augustan's old mother came to stay with her as she couldn't stay alone in the house.

I was always busy, buying groceries for her, assist her in shopping and go to banks and even routine checkups in hospitals.

Augustan's mother used to drink liquor at night. She takes two neat pegs of whiskey before having dinner. Sometimes she offered me a peg or two secretly. In those days I slept at Nina's guest room so that my parents wouldn't know that I have had liquor.

Two months passed. My desire for Nina was growing day by day.

One evening, I was pouring liquor to Augustan's mother. Nina was standing near me. She had a shot and offered me to have one.

Augustan's mother was happy and she drank more than her usual quota of two.

We had to carry her to her bed. When we were putting her to bed I hugged Nina. She didn't resist me.

Her mother in law was almost asleep in the bed.

My carnal desires were paramount. I was behind Nina and my arms around her belly.

My rod was awake and was pressing behind her.

How long we stood like that, I didn't know. But I felt her breaths became irregular and her lusty gasps steaming out.

My rod muscle was fully hard and tightly pressed to her ass and she pushed her ass back to keep the pressure intact.

"Let's go to my room." she whispered. I can see her breasts rising and lowing with each breath she took.

I freed her and we walked into her bedroom. She secured the door.

She was all horny and ready to explode.

She was wearing a sleeveless red satin silk nightwear.

We hugged again. I pressed her tits and ass at will. Her hands ran all over my body.

This was my lucky day. I have Nina with me ready to do anything. She is horny for my cock. Her round tits and butt are under attack by my hands. Soon I can see her all naked.

Uff, goose bumps filled my flesh.

Then she grabbed my cock. It was ready to burst out.

She pulled my trousers down and looked at the tent on my underwear. She smiled.

She pulled it down too and held my cock in her fist and stroked it. She did it very fast. I lost all my control. I wanted to do a lot of things, but…

Fuck…

That was a failure.

I came in a minute. My cream was on her nightwear and hands.

I really felt ashamed. I pulled my clothes up and unlocked the door. I silently went out of her house. I didn't even say a good night.

I felt very bad. I couldn't even get my cock inside her cunt.

I didn't know how I am going to face her again. I was proud of my long cock. I had the best cock among my friends.

And yet…

I failed her.

I felt like a loser.

I tried to avoid her the next whole day. I didn't even go there next two days.

But then one day Nina called for me. She wanted to buy something and I should take her in the bike.

I was worried what would have she thought of me about the fast ejection.

I had no other option but to face her. After the college I went there. Nina saw mw and went inside.

I talked to her mother in law. She complained that I ignored them and asked why I didn't visited them last few days.

I said I wasn't feeling very well. That's why I stayed at home.

She gave me some money. "My bottle is finished. If you are going out buy a liter for me."

Nina came to us; she was ready to go some purchase. She was wearing jeans and red t-shirt.

When we reached an abandoned area, she asked me to stop.

She hugged me from behind, pressing her tits against my back.

"That was your first time, I guess."

"Yes." I said, shyly.

"I need to buy some pills for protection. You must come today."

I couldn't believe her words. She didn't mind what happened with me that day.

"Relax your mind when you come. You can't enjoy a good fuck when your mind is disturbed."

She was stroking my cock. It was already aroused.

"You also have two pegs with mummy. That will help you." she whispered in my ears. Her stroking became strong. "I want to see it now."

I got off the bike and lowered my jeans and drawers. She came behind and stroked my cock until I came. This time I took few more minutes than the other day to explode.

Though it was still fast, I was feeling confident.

"Come on let's go." she said.

As she said I had two rounds of liquor and we made the old lady drink more. We carried her to the bed and were off to sleep soon.

Then we went to Nina's bedroom.

My heart was thumping fast. She was wearing the same red satin silk night wear she wore the other day.

I saw her hard nipples popping out of the night wear. She wasn't wearing any bra. I wondered whether she had panties too.

That amazing sight was enough for me for arousal.

I hugged her from the front and her boobs were against my chest. My hands trailed her back and went down to her butt.

She wasn't wearing panties too. She was all prepared tonight.

She understood my tension. She said. "Easy stallion, easy."

She unbuttoned my shirt and removed it. She licked my chest and nipples. Her tongue trailed down to my belly button.

I was experiencing the pleasure of a female seduction for the first time. She stripped my remaining clothes off.

My rod was standing erect and ready for action.

Nina gently caressed my cock and kissed its head. She licked the tip as her fingers nibbled my testicles. She took my whole rod into her mouth and fondled with passion. It went deep into her throat.

Uff, I was feeling the best pleasure in my life.

Was it the liquor, I don't know, but this time my cock didn't spit fire quickly. She was holding under the root of my cock tight to stop the flow. I felt my cream was stopped in its route to her mouth.

She was moaning as she ferried my hard muscle inside her mouth. Her speed increased and I produced sounds with ecstasy.

The moment she released her hold on my cock, it spit white fire. My rod was still in her mouth and I know the whole juice went inside her mouth.

I saw her swallow the whole cream and yet she was still fondling with it. My cock was getting soft but it seemed she didn't want to get it out of her mouth.

Once again I felt a little disappointed as I could insert my cock in her cunt.

I knew she also wanted that. She hasn't had a fuck for two months as Augustan has gone abroad. He will come back only after two years.

I was wondering what to do next.

She stood up and removed her night wear. I saw her, naked and aroused. Her dark beads were popped out. She was radiating heat of lust.

I could feel a spicy scent around her and I knew that was coming from her cunt.

Uff, what a sight!

That was the first time I was seeing a lady bare in front of me. Her tits were so beautiful and round. Her slim well curved features were driving me crazy. She has shaved her pubic hair. I knew in an instant that she shaved today after we came back from purchase.

I nibbled her round tits and licked all over her body. I kissed her like crazy on her tits, around nipples, belly, neck, chin, lips and behind her ears. My lips ran all over.

"Taste my cunt." She said.

She kept her legs wide open for me. I kneeled before her, my head was right against her spicy cunt, I got the strong heat emitting from her cunt.

Her cunt lips were pink and it was a sight to behold. My first encounter with a rosy cunt!

My whole body trembled with excitement.

"Kiss the clitoris first and lick on it. Slowly lick down to the slit. Aah." She moaned.

I did as I was told. I nibbled on her clit, trailed long enough to cover her entire cunt to her clit. She was wet and it tasted bitter sweet.

Her heat and aroma was biting into my nose.

I was experiencing a cunt for the first time but as she said later I did well for a first timer. I was weird and mad with my mouth and tongue.

I sucked one of the petals of her cunt and pulled gently with my lips.

"Aah." She gasped with lust and pleasure.

I felt her honey leaking into my mouth. I took it all. She wanted me to have her cunt honey.

She shook her ass with rhythm as the honey dripped into my mouth. She pushed my head closer to her cunt. I knew I should drink.

Tonight she was my sex teacher.

When she finished she released me and pulled me up. She went down and took my soft, sleeping cock in her mouth. She rubbed, licked, sucked and nibbled my cock and my balls.

I was hardening again.

She lay on the bed with her legs open.

Nina asked me to insert my rod and ram her.

She lifted her hips for me to enter her easily. She placed my cock at her entrance and asked me to push. Smoothly my cock went inside her wet cunt.

"Thrust hard; fuck me like you mean it."

I shook my body as I pushed harder and harder into her pussy. I felt a lot better now. I was growing in confidence.

I forced my cock deeper and deeper into her cunt as she rubbed her clit vigorously. My balls hit her perineal raphe repeatedly. I was focused on my cock getting deeper into her cunt. My body was supported with my hands stationed on both her sides.

My cock moved in and out of her cunt like a piston.

"I will come on top." She said.

We changed our positions. I lay on my back, my rod ready to shoot skywards.

She kissed my cock and nibbled my scrotum before sitting on top of me with my rod inside her.

Her hips danced over me, her butt hit over my pelvic area.

Each time her ass hit me, I could hear the soft thud.

She leaned onto me and kissed me. I grabbed her tits and started crushing them hard with my hands.

"Aah." She screamed.

Her pace increased and I applied more pressure on her boobs.

She did like an expert; she slowed down in between and wriggled her ass then again did faster.

"Fuck me from behind." She said as she climbed down. She bent forward with legs wide supporting her body against the wall.

I tried to insert into her ass.

"Not in my ass, put it in my pussy."

I rammed inside her cunt again and fucked her harder. I was comfortable in this position and pushed harder and harder inside her cunt.

I kissed the nape of her neck and licked behind her ears.

I can feel my cock scratching against her cunt walls.

She was horny and wild and made sweet pleasurable moans. I felt the moisture of her cunt on my cock as I guided my rod in and out with greater force.

I was leaning over her, one hand wrapping around her abdomen and other cupping one of her breasts.

She pushed her ass synchronizing with my rhythm and my cock went deeper inside hitting her cervix.

She rubbed her clit well with her fingers and the other hand was on the wall for support.

She gasped, moaned and groaned make me more wild. I felt her other boob dangling with the tempo.

"Ohh, that's it…that's how you do…" she encouraged me.

I filled her insides with my cream.

I slowly pushed to eject till the last drop and took my cock out.

She looked at me with satisfaction.

I know I did well. Her eyes were beaming.

"Sleep with me tonight, in my bed." she said.

I nod my head.

"Not just tonight but every night. I want a ride every day."

I promised her I will give her the ride to heaven every single night.

*****_____*****

******_______******

THE SNAKE GODDESS

THE NEIGHBOR

THE SEDUCED

THE SORCERER I

THE SORCERER II

THE SORCERER III

3 EROTIC STORIES

WIDOW'S DESIRE